# PETUNIA WOLF

## THE CASE CRACKER

### BOOK-2

AFSHEEN SHEIKH

ISBN
Paperback: 979-8-89588-957-2
Hardcase: 979-8-89632-450-8

# CONTENTS

Contents



## MASTERMIND

# Acknowledgements

I'd like to express my heartfelt gratitude to my wonderful parents, whose support and love have fueled my dreams.

I also want to thank my family, friends, teachers & readers who have played a significant role in shaping my journey. Your encouragement has been invaluable, and I'm deeply thankful.

From the bottom of my heart,

thank you all.

# WHO IS PETUNIA WOLF?

Meet the incredible Petunia Wolf, a 34-year-old detective and undercover agent in Furors, a province in Masikundra. With striking green eyes, radiant skin, and an amazing physique, she's not only famous but also the city's top detective, known for her daring and kind heart.

She believes, "Get your fears away and reach greater heights!"

# HAUNTED BY
# SHADOWS

# CHAPTER 1

# WHISPERS OF THE DARK

She was sweating, she could feel her heart thumping in her chest. She was in a quiet, deserted alley enclosed by the horror of the night. There was no light, just sheer darkness. She could hear a piercing scream but she couldn't move, she couldn't do anything. She had failed her profession, failed herself. She felt like the most useless and worthless person on the planet. She couldn't stop a crime being a detective and agent herself. What was the point of her existence? She didn't know anymore. She wanted to end it all but the thought of her daughter and best friend stopped her every time.

This is a tale of the previous year which had changed the course of her life and of those close to her:

It was a bright morning. The sun gleamed through the windows of Petunia's townhouse and a dainty breeze blew through Furors. Petunia set out for work early and got straight to paperwork as soon as she reached. She had no time to waste. A month-long vacation hadn't done her a favor at all. Now, she had three huge piles of files to tackle. She swiftly read through the cases that happened in her absence and looked through other confidential files of high importance. She was glad to see that the crime rate in Furors was now reducing thanks to the awareness she had created over the past three years.

Petunia started updating her records and spreadsheets and before she knew it, it was night time. Petunia was exhausted and realization hit her. She hadn't eaten anything since breakfast and her tummy was grumbling. Everyone else had left.

Petunia got herself some coffee before starting to drive home. She decided to take a shortcut and entered a narrow alleyway.

There were small shops and restaurants, all closed by then. Not a single light was turned on. As she drove further, there was a small cafeteria that was amazingly still open. Petunia entered to get some takeaway burgers.

But, to her astonishment, there was no one there. She entered the kitchen to recheck and she saw a figure in the freezer room where all the patties and bread were stored. It was a teenager weeping and shivering. She looked frightened and screamed when she saw Petunia. She closed her mouth with her hands and tears rolled down her bony cheeks. She was traumatized by something, or perhaps, someone. Something was very wrong.

Petunia confronted the young woman but as she stepped forward, the girl got up and kept moving further and further away until she hit the wall behind her. She fell to the floor and tugged at her hair whimpering, unable to utter a single word. Just as Petunia got close, she started to scream, "Get out of here. It's not safe. You don't want to be here. Please just leave, NOW!" Petunia reassured her but she didn't pay heed and kept insisting for her to leave. She revealed her identity and took the girl out of the freezer. She was shivering and her skin started to turn blue. She had hypothermia. Petunia rushed to get some cloth from her car and covered her up to give warmth. She had to be rushed to the hospital. The teenager begged that she wouldn't go to the hospital and that she would rather die than leave the place.

Petunia was confused. She called her family doctor who came immediately and assisted the girl. She lay down on the floor covered in layers of warm blankets. Just as she was about to rest, she shrieked suddenly, sending a shiver down Petunia's spine. The girl pointed at the café's window but there was no one there. Petunia stared for some time and noticed a dark shadow there. When she went out to check, there was no one. The shadow had vanished into thin air. This was very strange.

Petunia offered the girl to come to her home for the night but she refused the proposal saying that she would get killed. Petunia tried asking her about her potential killer but the girl never answered. She remained quiet, not daring to speak. She whispered to Petunia, "Please don't tell anyone about your visit here, about me or about this place. I plead to you." Petunia agreed for now but she knew she had to do something. She knew the girl was in serious danger.

Petunia ruled out the possibilities of the crime type. It was probably assault, abuse or human trafficking but she wasn't sure. The case needed further investigation. She decided to personally solve the case since the teenager wanted to keep it private. Petunia began spying on the cafeteria every day when she returned from work. The cafeteria always had a 'CLOSED' sign hung on the door but somehow, the lights remained on throughout the day. She knew someone was in there and the person was targeting the young girl and possibly, others as well.

At ten in the night, the alley was dark and gloomy, no sign of life except the chittering little crickets. That day, the shop that was always lit was empty, no girl, no mysterious shadow. There were no vehicles around either, no clue of their whereabouts. The café looked like it had been abandoned for a decade with cobwebs sprawling all over the place and the floor covered in blooming moss. It looked quite old and rusty, not like anything she'd seen before.

Petunia entered cautiously and a horrendous stench of rotting meat caught her almost making her puke. She entered the freezer room where she had first seen the girl but lo! There was not a single soul. Petunia wondered where the stench came from and she started to map out the place using her senses.

She discovered the place where the reek was strongest. It was coming from an old tap that seemed unused for quite some time. Petunia opened the tap and blood trickled from within. Petunia jumped back aghast. Her thoughts started swirling and she imagined the worst scenarios possible. She couldn't move for a bit but she knew she had to be brave. She went to the source of the tap water, to the tank above the café. She opened the lid and was relieved to see a dead, rotting mouse. It was no human blood; it was clearly not a murder but the criminal definitely wanted to make it look like one.

He had erased all his footprints and traces of his victims. This was going to be a difficult case, one unlike anything she had ever been through before. Things weren't the same anymore. There could be a psychopath roaming across Furors searching for his prey but she could never be too sure. What if she was hallucinating that day, what if there was no girl, what if everything she experienced was a nightmare? Petunia's head ached trying to find an answer but she knew she couldn't give up. She had to find the truth.

Petunia relaxed her bulging temples and tried to massage her head to calm herself down. She tried looking for clues because she believed that come what may, a criminal always makes a mistake. Petunia entered the kitchen and started searching all the cabinets.

There was nothing, but at the ones at the deep ends, the interior of a particular cabinet looked new and spotless. Petunia punched it numerous times only to unlock a terminal, a secret hallway. The entrance was tiny, too small for her to fit in there. She had to call in somebody to help. She didn't want to tell the detective office just yet until she was sure of the authenticity of the event so she called her trusty companion, her daughter Diana. She was slim and could fit in small spaces. Petunia was risking her life and her daughter's but Diana agreed to join her. This was something that was to be kept between just the two of them.

Diana walked to the old café with her phone. She wore a grey hoodie to protect her identity and was swift in her movements. She found her mother sweltering and checked out the little entrance before reassuring her. She was sure that she could easily squeeze through the narrow gap. Petunia assisted Diana as she set foot and crawled on her elbows, forward into the long tunnel. Diana carried a small camera with her and recorded everything she saw on the way. As she crawled deeper and out of sight, Petunia heard a loud thud and she yelled to her, "DIANA! Are you alright, what happened?" Petunia heard a sigh.

Diana was alright but she had discovered a hidden room that was way bigger than the tunnel. It was deserted but there were boot prints on the muddy ground. They looked like they had been made just a few hours ago. The soil was moist and something lit up the path. Their link of communication snapped as they couldn't hear each other due to the long distance that now separated them. Diana stepped forward unafraid.

Petunia was extremely worried at this point and she kept screaming for Diana to come back but she stood her guard and moved ahead. That's when she noticed an operating camera on the ceiling whirring at her and flashing red lights. It had detected her and whoever owned the place could watch her every move. Diana hid her face in a jiffy and ran back to where she came from but a figure came in her way blocking the exit. Diana shrieked as loud as she could but she couldn't escape. She saw the man who held her. He had a strange mask covering his face and Diana was scared for her life. She bit his hand and kicked him as hard as she could. The man was stunned and became immobile for some time.

Diana grabbed the opportunity to get back to the tunnel back to her mother. She roared,

*"CODE RED, CODE RED!"* Petunia quickly found an old mop and held it to give support to Diana. The man was back to his senses and started to tug at Diana's legs. No wonder he was strong. Petunia resisted the force and pulled her daughter out safely. Diana was hyperventilating. Petunia felt like the worst mother ever. She had almost killed her own daughter. She apologized and took her home to get some rest. Diana was a lion and she recovered from the trauma in minutes. Now, Petunia knew for sure that a villain existed in the whispers of the shadows awaiting his next victim. The main question now was, "What did he do with the people he caught?"

# CHAPTER 2

# CODE RED

Petunia immediately called her senior, Odila Matthew. It was two in the morning but she didn't care. This was a matter of everyone's safety and security. She had to act quickly before someone else's life was in danger. This was a matter of urgency and the public had to know about it to protect themselves.

Odila was annoyed by the late call but as soon as she heard about the incident, she was alarmed and got up with a jerk. She directed Petunia to report to the office as soon as possible. They met thirty minutes later. Odila was concerned for the safety of the youth and she immediately contacted media agencies to spread the news. She instructed everyone to stay put and not step out of their houses after seven in the night. The team had to start investigating immediately. Petunia was made the leader.

The investigation team explored every nook and crook of the café, especially the area where Diana almost got caught. As they opened the peculiar cabinet, they were astonished to find that there was no tunnel there, not anymore. It had been covered by a large metal piece and upon unscrewing it, they discovered that there was just solid rock all the way in- no tunnels, no rooms. The criminal was definitely smart. He knew danger was coming his way.

Petunia thought otherwise. The tunnel could have most likely been shifted somewhere else, somewhere in the surrounding vicinity. The team headed towards an abandoned park nearby. It had an eerie feel to it, no light. The ground was moist and had foreign sand particles, a type of sand that couldn't be found in Furors. This was a breakthrough for them, they were sure that someone suspicious was in there. The team of seven members split up. They explored every corner of the creepy park. Some places were so dark that they needed night vision glasses to see.

One of the members, named Farnon, had found something. He communicated with the others through his walkie talkie, "Team, come in. I've found a hollow piece of land. There's something underneath here. Report to the east zone near the swings. Over." The others answered, "Roger that. Reporting now." As each member started to gather at the meeting point, they couldn't seem to find Farnon anywhere. The members began to yell for him, "Farnon, where are you? FARNON!"

And while everyone was busy searching for him, another team member called Gale got nabbed too. Now, they had two members missing. They were worried and some suggested that they abort the mission. Petunia did not agree, "They are part of the team. You can't just abandon them here. They could be in grave danger, something bad could happen to them! Please, let's search for them." Everyone agreed but two of them were still skeptical.

Just as they were devising an action plan, they felt the presence of someone else and a shadow walked past them. They knew it was the criminal hunting for his next victim.

Petunia said with a quiver of guilt and grief in her voice, "There's no time for words. We need to act now. Stick together everyone. We can't afford the loss of another team member." They started digging the hollow piece of land. A latch lay before them. It was protected by a lock but not any regular lock. It was one that required the owner's iris scan. The team was baffled. They didn't know what to do now. They had no choice but to step back and wait.

They hid in the bushes behind an old slide, close enough that they could see if someone approached the latch. Petunia looked around and noticed something moving in the distance. She told everyone to stay back and moved towards the object on her own. It was a shed covered in dead leaves and fallen branches. This wasn't anything special but just as Petunia looked around it, she found a camera, a fully functioning 360° camera. It was watching her and every team member of theirs. The criminal was watching every move of theirs. He was stalking them.

Now, Petunia knew it wasn't safe for them to stay there anymore. They had to seek refuge, hide before he caught them. Just as she was about to return and warn her teammates, something caught her from behind and she felt a damp cloth on her face. A strong scent of chloroform struck her unconscious. The last thing she remembered was someone dragging her through the grassy fields.

Her teammates waited for hours but she never returned and nor did the criminal come by. Their best guess was that she had been taken too, gone. Due to a vast majority's agreement, they fled the place and terminated their undertaking. Word spread and news reporters stormed the Furors office. Odila was questioned severely about the disappearances but she had no answers. Deep down, she knew Petunia would save herself and everyone that was in danger yet she doubted her beliefs because fate could turn around anytime. She was deeply concerned.

Petunia, on the other hand, hadn't regained consciousness yet. The effect of the chloroform was too strong on her. The criminal had given her a very high dosage and had injected her with something worse.

Petunia's blood pressure increased, she was drenched in sweat and her body started to shake. She opened her eyes to see extremely bright lights surrounding her. She covered her eyes with her hand and tried to stand but she couldn't, as if she was paralyzed. She wasn't tied up nor was she restricted movement. Her best guess was that he had injected a chemical called curare into her legs. It was a poisonous substance that could possibly result in her death. She needed the antidote, now! She couldn't breathe, she was suffocating and before she knew it, she was knocked out again...

# CHAPTER 3

# DEATHBED

Petunia woke up and realized she had been shifted to another room, now completely dark with not a single source of light. She tried to move her leg and surprisingly, she could. She had been given the antidote but she still felt weird. She couldn't move as easily as she could before. She felt a sharp pain in her ankle. She reached down to touch it and felt a thick, slimy substance. As she pulled it to her nose, she understood it was her blood. Someone had wounded her. As Petunia stood up and hopped on one leg, she noticed she was in a tiny room, like one at the mental asylum where violent patients were kept locked. She shouted at the top of her lungs, "Is anyone out there? Who are you? Why are you doing this? Get me out of here!"

Suddenly, the door opened and the same black figure stood there. It was a man and he was wearing a surgical mask. He said, "Shut up twit or I'll kill ya. I ain't answering your stupid questions, you get me?" Petunia confronted the man, "Who do you think you are kidnapping all these innocent people? I don't care if you kill me but free all these lives!" The man got angry and pulled Petunia out of the room by her hair, "Ya really want to die today, huh? And, I am not freeing any of my rats, understand woman? You are a mere puppet just like everyone else here." Petunia was shocked. What did he mean by puppet?

The hefty man grabbed Petunia and threw her to the floor. He had scientific equipment with him which he allegedly used for his victims. Petunia was scared but she got up and knocked him out using a simple trick but just as she did, an alarm rang echoing through the corridors of the underground place. The man exploded into tiny bits caused by an in-built defense mechanism made to cause injury to the attacker.

Petunia stepped back as he caught on fire. Petunia cleared her vision and realized it was a humanoid robot. She was perplexed. How could a piece of metal act and feel like a human being? The scientist behind this was definitely a madman. Petunia extinguished the flames with a fire extinguisher nearby and started to walk around the place. She tied a cloth to her ankle and moved ahead.

She saw numerous rooms just like the one she was placed in. She knew there were people in there who were most likely getting harmed and tortured just like her a moment ago. She had to find the control center. She had to free everyone. She started to mentally map out the place. She needed to navigate it in case there was more danger ahead of her. As she scrutinized the place, the words of the teenager echoed at the back of her head. Her heart told her she was here, trapped in one of these rooms.

The entire place seemed like a never-ending puzzle. Everything looked the same and she was constantly monitored by hundreds of cameras. She could never imagine even in her wildest dreams that Furors could have such a vast underground criminal network. However, she was sure of one thing, the culprit definitely wasn't from Furors. The foreign sand particles explained that.

Petunia found an unusual door with the enigmatic numbers 011 on it. She snapped the door open only to realize it was an obstacle course. The entire pathway was filled with beartraps with distances of less than a meter. There were knives and needles on the floor, just lying there. She spotted another room in the distance and as her vision cleared, she saw that it was the control room. She was barefoot, she had no shoes on. The criminal or as it seemed now, criminals had taken them away. Petunia was stuck there; she couldn't move forward. The trail that lay ahead was too risky. She could risk herself and the lives of other victims. She had to step back on this one and think of how to get through the obstacles but she couldn't. She felt a strong ache at the back of her head and just as she turned, someone hit her hard. Her forehead started to bleed and she saw a blurry figure before thudding to the ground.

About an hour later, she found herself in one of those dark cells again but she could feel something was different. As she was recovering from the pain, a bright light flashed at her and that's when she clearly saw where she was. She was tied to a chair but not an ordinary one. She was held down by heavy metal chains on a dentist chair. She couldn't move and squirmed. Just then, a woman entered the room wearing a surgical mask and gloves. She looked unreal, like a real robot. Her eyes were glassy and metallic but she had the features of a human. She moved in jerks and had a bizarre way of holding things.

She had an injection in her hand filled with a thick, purple liquid. Petunia tried to resist but moving even an inch was impossible. The robot approached her and injected the liquid into her arm. Petunia was in pain but in vain, the robot had no feelings. The robot left her there back in the dark. Petunia started to sense change in her body. Her nerves were popping and she felt her body temperature drop significantly. She was shivering and her temperature continued to drop. Her skin changed color. Her fair complexion started turning blue then purple. She was cold. She had hypothermia just like that teenager. The robot had left her to die. Petunia closed her eyes and waited patiently for help but she no longer could. It was beyond her body's capability. The heart monitor next to her showed her heart rate dropping constantly. *BEEP...BEEP...BEEEEEEEEEP.* It turned into a straight line. She was gone, perhaps forever. It was only a miracle that could save her now.

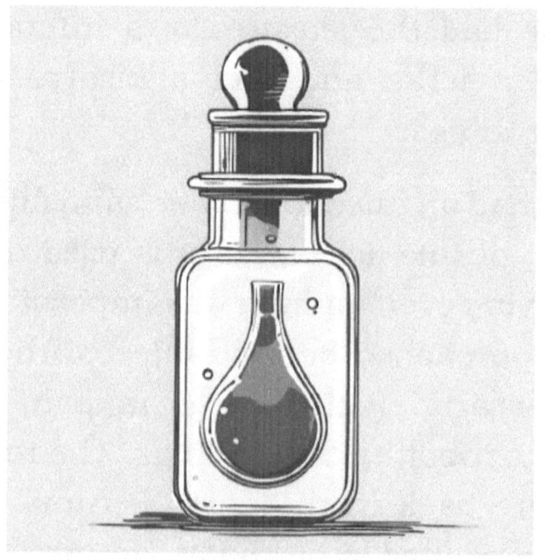

Suddenly, someone entered the scene and injected something into Petunia's arm, an antidote. Whoever it was thought there was still hope left. The antidote was yellow in color and it repelled the purple infection that still flowed within her body. It was a marvel!

Her heart rate started to increase and her body temperature was eventually returning back to normal. She opened her eyes slowly, confused. There were no chains on her and no popping nerves. It was like nothing ever happened.

Petunia comprehended that the victims were being experimented on. Some mad scientist was on the loose, and his freedom could risk the lives of the entire nation. He was a psycho ready to ruin the health of many. He had to be stopped before it was too late.

# CHAPTER 4

# CONTROL CENTER

Petunia had to reach the control center in order to get closer to the criminal or catch him once and for all. His AI minions were cruel but Petunia believed that he was crueler for making them do this, for making those heartless creatures torture innocent people with his crazy ideas.

Petunia concluded that there could be more types of diseases in his lab waiting to be experimented on his 'lab rats'. He had turned this into an underground base in order to carry out his killer trials. These people had to be rescued, taken out of this living hell alive. The madman could've been the one who had saved her or just another robot, maybe. She wouldn't know until she got to the control center.

Petunia had to devise strategies to get in there without hurting herself or alerting the criminal. She needed to find something sturdy that could at least protect her from the knives and needles. She started looking for thick pieces of metal or wood and she saw the heavy chains that were placed on her in the distance. She started crafting some soles out of them, knotting the chains together and creating a strap strong enough to hold her foot. It was hard to walk in thanks to its heavy weight but at least, her safety was guaranteed. The metal clanked on the floor heavily. The sound echoed through the empty corridors. She walked slowly and steadily.

Petunia reached the entrance of 011. It looked scarier than ever. Petunia had to be very cautious for the next ten meters. The path was long and there could be other unseen obstacles.

As soon as Petunia stepped away from the beartraps, she triggered something and a series of axes opened up from the ceiling, slicing the air and waiting to slice her too. Petunia had to be super careful now. She had to be mindful of the beartraps as well as the axes. The madman had placed them very close so that it could deter the victim's concentration and lead to a higher chance of fatality. Thank God Petunia had an alert mind and agility. She moved smoothly and swiftly like water, being watchful of both the beartraps and the flying axes. The person behind this was definitely insane, a terrifier, a murderer and a maniac.

The door to the control room glimmered in front of Petunia's eyes. She kicked it open with her heavy metal slippers. The entire room was covered with screens displaying footage from the surveillance cameras. It seemed like the person monitoring them had gone for a little break. His coffee mug was still warm, he was definitely nearby and this time, it was undoubtedly a human.

Petunia hid in a corner awaiting his return. She was in position to capture him. She had untied one of the metal chains. The man entered with an expression of disbelief on his face. He looked around and deciphered that someone had barged in and intruded his workplace. He ran for the exit knowing he was threatened. Petunia waited for the right moment and sprang into action. She threw the chains like a lasso and caught him by the neck. She pulled him hard and tied him to his chair. The questioning began.

*Petunia:* "What is your name and why are you doing this?"

*Man:* "I won't answer any of your questions lady. How dare you barge into my office?!"

*Petunia:* "I ask the questions here. If you don't answer me, I'll be right glad to throw you into prison."

*Man:* "PRISON!? OH GOD I'M SO SCARED. (starts chuckling) Do you know who Mastermind is?

*Petunia:* "Well, tell me now. I need information of your so-called 'Mastermind'."

*Man:* "I am not going to reveal anything no matter what you try to do. You're just a mere woman. What in the world do you think you can do, huh?"

*Petunia:* "Well, I just showed you what I can do. Look who's being petty tied up in a chair. I can do things way worse mister. (punches him and steals his gun pointing it to his head)

*Now, answer me! Or do you want to lose your life?"*

*Man: "Woah, woah... calm down, I was just kidding superwoman. (in a hushed voice) I'll tell you if you promise to get me out of here alive."*

*Petunia: "What do you mean?"*

*Man: "Shush, listen to me! (whispering) There are cameras in this room that the Mastermind can see. He could be watching and hearing us. He is most probably alert by now and could be sending his robotic army. We need to get out of here. He can't view footage of the other rooms unless he pays very close attention. Act along with me, now!"*

*Petunia: "Okay, this better not be a trap."*

*Man: "Who do you think you are? Get out of here. Take this thing off me."*

*Petunia: "I'm so sorry. I thought you were a bad guy. Hang on, let me free you. (takes off the metal chain)."*

*Man: "Alright. Get movin' now. Your assigned room's that way. Don't make me repeat myself."*

Petunia played along and followed the man to her room. She had taken off her heavy metal flip flops. Her leg hurt but her concern for others didn't allow her to step back. The man led her out through a secret exit, not filled with violent weapons. The man started to tell her everything from the start.

"My name's Noa Alfred. I come from a small town in Franca. I have two daughters in Furors. I shifted here a year ago in search of work but you see, I am not really qualified. I dropped out of college; my parents had no money at the time. My family lived in poverty. My kids were always picked on at school because of the way they dressed.

Two months ago, Mastermind found me in misery. He offered me a job here on one condition that I wouldn't tell anyone about it, not even my wife. It was hard but I agreed. The job at the control center paid me really well.

Just a month ago, he started bringing in people to the lab and my daughter was one of them. I protested, tried to fight him but he throttled and almost took my life, and threatened to take my daughter Nikki's too. I was helpless, I couldn't do anything. I had to give in to his commands. I felt bad for everyone. I wanted to free them but Mastermind always had an eye on me. He let Nikki go but threatened to kill my family if I did anything wrong."

Petunia felt terrible for the man. Though it all seemed like an emotional fairytale at the beginning, the part where he spoke about Nikki touched her heart. She could understand his pain. She said, "Noa, what has happened to you is not right, it's wrong beyond words. Thank you for the information but could you explain what exactly happens here and who Mastermind truly is? I will try my best to save all the people trapped here."

Noa replied, "Experiments! Inhumane experiments! All these young, healthy people are injected with lethal infections and antidotes are tested on them. Some did not even make it out alive. He hides them, dumps them after doing hundreds of trails on them. Mastermind, well, no one knows how he looks. I've never seen him without a mask, really. Some of my colleagues say his name is Jordane but no one knows for sure."

Petunia understood that Jordane was someone who took advantage of the vulnerable, desolate folks and forced them into working with him. He was brutal, vicious and had no mercy for anyone. He had to be caught but with no contact with the intelligence team, there was less Petunia could do.

She asked for Noa's help. They could save everyone together.

# Chapter 5

# Ambuscade

Petunia needed Noa to get to the control center and unlock all the doors of the underground lab. They needed the victims to be let out but there was a problem, opening all the doors would sound an alarm and alert Mastermind. Petunia understood and asked, "Well, is there a way to turn off all systems here?" Noa thought for a minute and answered, "Yes there is but doing so would cut off ventilation and release methane into the air as the lab is detected as abandoned. Mastermind is too intelligent. In case, the authorities try to get close to him, he would kill them with poisonous gas. If we do this, everyone will die in a matter of seconds."

This was not a viable solution. They had to unlock the doors one by one now. That was their safest choice. Noa was unsure, though he worked there for quite some time, he couldn't navigate around very well. Mastermind had made it that way, like a maze. He said that there were approximately two hundred and seventy rooms in total, each housing at least one victim. There was a lot to do and very little time. Before opening all the gates, they had to find an exit that would lead the victims out safely and so, the hunt commenced.

Noa knew five emergency exits across the entire lab but these could only be triggered by a fire or smoke, to the minimum. They had to find something to ignite. Petunia thought that a robot would be great. She asked for a glass of water. Noa searched for a while and found a bottle of water hidden in one of the cabinets. Petunia grabbed it and threw it at the robot. The water sprayed on it causing a short circuit and a small fire.

The fire alarm set off and all the doors unlocked one by one. The victims came out tired and dizzy, including the girl she had met that day. They needed to be helped out. Noa and Petunia gathered everyone into a room near the exit. It opened up into a dark alley. After two hours of strenuous efforts, everyone was safely assembled in Room 102. But there was a huge problem now.

They heard mechanical whirring in the distance and loud metallic footsteps clattered on the floor. Petunia held everyone together, protecting them at the forefront. She urged, "Stay back everyone! Don't move." She stepped forward with caution observing her surroundings intricately. She peeked through the door and saw an army- a huge, ginormous army of around a hundred giga-sized robots, all towering to the ceiling. Their necks were crooked, their blank eyeballs eerily staring at the floor.

With a buzz and a flash of light, the robotic heads rose in unison, almost as if someone was controlling them. They constantly repeated, "Danger! Danger! Danger! Patients escaping!" Their eyes lit bright red and they locked Petunia as their target, flashing lasers upon her body. Petunia had to flee now but also allow the others to do so. She had to use the method she had applied before just this time, she had to act faster.

She called Noa and asked him to get the water dispenser from Room 102. He strenuously carried it and walked towards Petunia. He doused the robots and they began to explode one by one setting ablaze the lab. Petunia started to evacuate everyone. At the end, it was only Petunia and Noa left in the hellhole suffering in the heat.

An announcement came over the PA speakers, "Doors closing...Lab in quarantine." Noa pushed Petunia out the closing exit. She escaped but Noa didn't. The flames swallowed him and a scream of agony bellowed through the air. Petunia was still in shock from what had happened. All the other patients came to her, all worried and in trauma from Noa's death.

Petunia felt like the worst person in the world. She was right there yet she could do nothing to help him, save his life. He had a family to go back to- a beautiful wife and two eager children. How would she answer them? What would she tell them about him? These thoughts were consuming her inside out. But she had to save the others.

She rushed them all to a hospital but couldn't find the courage to get herself treated after what had happened. She decided to walk back home. She was sweating, with burns all over her body and she could feel her heart thumping in her chest. She was in the quiet, deserted alley enclosed by the horror of the night. There was no light, just sheer darkness.

She could hear the piercing scream resounding in her ear but she couldn't move, she couldn't do anything. She had been pushed to safety and Noa had sacrificed himself.

She felt like she had failed her profession, failed herself. She was the most useless and worthless person on the planet. She couldn't stop a crime being a detective and agent herself. What was the point of her existence? She didn't know anymore. She wanted to end everything once and for all but she couldn't.

She knew she had to fight for him and do justice to his soul. She had to take on the challenge to find Mastermind and end him forever...not just for him but for the safety of her nation and her people.

# THE QUEST TO JUSTICE

# Chapter 1

# The Funeral

"With humble acceptance of God's will, we announce the passing of Noa on 16th of June 2020. He was the beloved son of Mr. and Mrs. Alfred, husband of Levana Smith Alfred, and father of Nikki and Camilla Alfred. The funeral of this brave personality shall now commence with a speech by Petunia Wolf, the detective who he spent his last moments with," said Priest Raymond.

The atmosphere was one of gloom, terror and utmost grief. All the souls present in the room were dressed in black, their eyes were filled with tears and their hearts, with memories of him. His casket glowed in the dim lights; his remains wrapped neatly in white cloth.

Petunia was unkempt, she had gone through rigorous interrogation since the past three days. Shame and guilt chewed on her, not ready to let go. Petunia was proven innocent but she knew deep down that she could've saved him and been the one to give away her life for his. His family stared at her with a look of dread and rage. Petunia could not find the courage to look them in the eye. She started to tear up and she sobbed, burying her face in her coat sleeve. Once her name was called for the opening speech of the funeral, she wiped her eyes and stood up gently, walking face down. She got onto the podium and commenced looking down,

"Ladies and Gentlemen,

We are here today with heavy hearts to honour Noa Alfred, a true hero whose bravery saved so many lives. I'm overwhelmed with guilt, knowing I was right there but couldn't save him.

*Pauses, tears welling up.*

I only knew Noa for a few hours, but in that short time, his courage and kindness shone so brightly. On that terrible day, he didn't hesitate. He put everyone else first. I can't stop replaying those moments, wishing

I could have done something, anything, to save him.

*Voice breaking, pauses to weep.*

To Noa's parents: your son was incredible. His bravery and kindness were evidence of how you raised him. I am so deeply sorry. I wish I could have done more.

To Levana, Nikki, and Camilla: Noa loved you more than words can say. He spoke about you with such pride and joy. I can't imagine your pain, but please know his love and spirit are always with you.

*Pauses, tears streaming down her face.*

Noa's legacy of heroism and love will live on in our hearts forever. We will never forget his loss.

*Struggles to speak, voice choked with emotion.*

Noa Alfred, thank you for your incredible sacrifice. You are our hero. Rest in peace. I will carry the weight of your loss with me for the rest of my life.

*Breaks down, crying openly.*

Thank... *sobs...*you..."

Petunia stepped down, bawling her eyes out. She fell to the floor and wrapped her arms around her. Noa's wife approached her and sat next to her, almost trying to comfort her. Her voice quivered, "Petunia, I learnt from the others.... who were also trapped back there that you weren't at fault. I may have been mad at you, but you and Noa.... were true warriors.... and I know you wanted to save everyone. My man was tremendously brave and it was his decision.... to sacrifice his life and it's not your fault. You couldn't even comprehend what happened to you for moments. I feel your guilt... but I think it's time you settle down. It's an enormous loss for us but we have...to (sobs) move on...." She whimpered and wailed next to her longing for her beloved other half who was now gone forever.

"Levana," Petunia whispered, her voice trembling like fragile glass. "I... I wish I could believe that. But the weight of his sacrifice... it's crushing."

*Petunia takes a breather and wipes her tears.*

"I can't shake the feeling that I failed him, failed everyone. If only I had been faster, smarter... maybe he'd still be here."

*Her breath hitches, tears flowing freely now.*

"Fate... it feels so cruel, Levana. To snatch him away, to leave us all here... broken."

"Petunia," she began softly, "I understand your pain, your guilt. But please, listen to me. Noa wouldn't want you to carry this burden alone. He wouldn't want you to blame yourself for what happened. You were both heroes that day, facing danger with courage and determination.

We may never understand why these things happen, why fate can be so merciless. But we can find strength in each other. Noa's sacrifice was not in vain, Petunia. He saved countless lives, and his legacy will live on in the hearts of all who knew him."

*She squeezes Petunia's hand gently, offering a small, sad smile.*

"We'll get through this together. I know you'll do justice to him, Petunia. I believe in you. Come on, let's take a seat."

They both headed to the hall and took their seats beside each other. Nikki and Camilla were only eight years old. They remained quiet throughout and mourned silently. It was time for his burial. They looked from afar as his remains were carried away and lay to rest. His gravestone read, "NOA ALFRED, THE BRAVE HERO OF FURORS, 1988-2020."

News spread like wildfire and people brought bouquets of flowers to send peace and blessings upon the humble and heroic soul. The news channels were flooded with stories of him, and Petunia was called for interviews several times. She attended every one of them to tribute his valour multiple times. She decided that it was now time to embark on the quest of justice. The news of his death must've reached Mastermind by then and his threat to harm Noa's family still lingered. Noa hadn't done anything wrong but, in his eyes, he had. He had set Mastermind's lab on fire and freed hundreds of his 'lab rats'.

His family could be killed and they needed to be protected. Petunia immediately dispatched three of her most qualified officers to guard their home and his children. Officer Stacee accompanied them to school and Officer Alishia and Sydnie stayed at his home and took care of Levana who was in despair. Mastermind (or possibly Jordane) needed to be found at the earliest before he made his next move.

# Chapter 2

# The Search Begins

Mastermind's targets were at random. Did he take in anyone he'd find or did he want someone special, someone extraordinary for his experiments? Out of the 275 people Petunia and Noa had saved, eighty-eight of them were below the age of 18 and the rest of them ranged from twenty to thirty-five years of age. One thing was for sure, he wanted young and healthy victims as Noa had mentioned. It was now important for her to find his whereabouts and his next 'lab rats'.

Petunia conducted a survey for the people she had saved to understand where they lived, where they came from and what they did. The results were extremely shocking.

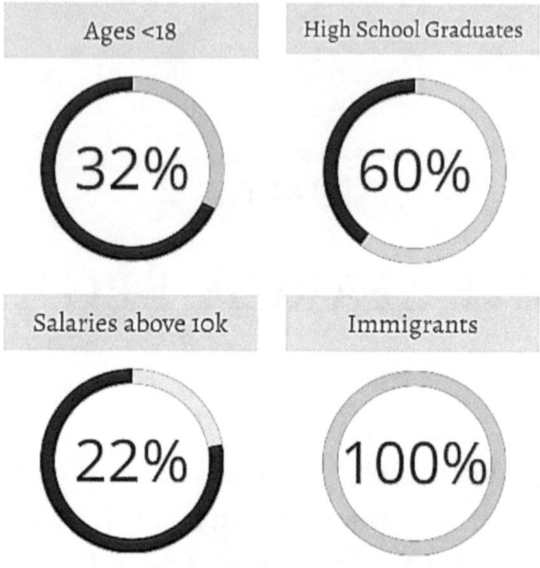


The survey revealed something intriguing. Mastermind's targets were all immigrants, hailing from nations such as Franca, Beligia, Suncham, and Litnich. These nations, while geographically adjacent to Masikundra, lacked its level of development and integration which was why these populations were weaker and more vulnerable. These countries were struggling with underdevelopment and limited resources, thus many sought refuge in Furors, drawn by the promise of a better life. It seemed as if Mastermind was taking advantage of this fact and exploiting their health.

The immigrants made up a significant portion of Furor's population and economy. Most worked as community helpers and some of them attained high positions with sky-high income through their hard-work. Many children studied in Furor's schools and universities and the people there were glad to have them, always welcoming them with open hands and a big heart.

Someone exclusively targeting them was devastating. Mastermind seemed to have a bigger target after this and what he would do next was unclear.

Petunia had to protect these immigrants as well as find out about Jordane. A public announcement was made once again that all residents, regardless of being a citizen or an immigrant, must stay home after seven PM and not step out unless there is an emergency. The warning was now enforced as a temporary rule until the matter settled. The people were given vague information to not cause chaos and interfere with legal practices.

However, they sensed something was wrong and started to retaliate. Groups of people were out on the streets and began to protest. The news was all over social media. People held up signs and posters with messages like, "Transparency Now!" and "We demand answers, not silence!" Petunia didn't know what to do. She chose to appear in a media broadcast and sent a message to everyone in the city:

"Good evening, citizens of Furors. This is Petunia speaking to you in light of recent events. I understand your concerns and frustrations regarding the recent measures implemented for public safety.

I want to assure you that your well-being is our top priority. We are working diligently to address the situation and provide you with the transparency and answers you deserve.

There could be a psychopath running loose in Furors targeting children and young adults to perform perilous and vicious scientific experiments. More than 200 people have been affected already.

I urge everyone to remain calm and cooperative during this time. The temporary curfew is a precautionary measure intended to ensure the safety of all residents.

I promise to keep you informed as we navigate through this together. Your patience and understanding are invaluable as we work towards resolution.

Thank you, and stay safe."

This tremendously helped in de-escalating the situation as everyone started to return back home and stay put. The people of Furors had trust in Petunia's efforts and they decided to cooperate. At the same time, they were also concerned for the safety of their children and their own so they didn't quite have a choice.

Petunia could now begin the investigation with everyone's help and support. She assumed that Jordane was from Masikundra who just hated others or had a weird and violent knack for science. His end would mean everyone's safety and security. Petunia contacted universities and requested a name list of the people who took science majors in the past years. Upon compiling the results, she shortlisted four plausible suspects:

1. Mr. Jordane Smith

2. Ms. Jordyn Taylor

3. Mr. Jordane Blake

4. Mr. Jordynn Parker

She found that these names possessed a similar tone to the alleged psycho. All these personalities had to be looked through thoroughly. She began with *Mr. Jordane Smith*, the closest match.

His address was around two kilometres from her home. Petunia arrived at his house and knocked thrice only to discover from his neighbours that he had left the country with his family five years ago and no one lived there anymore. Definitely couldn't have been the one behind all of this.

Her next suspect was *Mr. Jourdan Blake.* His lab was situated in the depths of Furors Forest. He was quite a mysterious man. However, he was known for his groundbreaking discoveries in organic compounds. Petunia got her tech team to hack into his lab's database and discovered that he was working on a top-secret project the night before the incident. She decided to confront him for more details.

Jourdan was a bizarre man. He was old, with two specks of white hair on his head. His lab had a ten-step security system so no one could physically enter. But Petunia had a strong intelligence team that hacked into his system with ease. Petunia asked Jourdan, "Good day sir! I am Petunia and I'd like to ask you a few questions. May I get ten minutes of your time?" The "great" scientist refused and slammed the door on her face. Petunia was infuriated but she controlled herself and knocked again.

She knew about his dark past. He had illegally smuggled banned materials into the country to carry out his experiments. There was a case on him in the past but he bribed the judge and was set free. Petunia firmly said, "Alright, professor. You've got two choices: start talking, or I'll expose every dirty little secret you've tried to keep hidden. Your reputation will be in shambles, and trust me, your career won't survive the fallout. So, what's it gonna be?" He opened the door for a moment to say, "I don't care kid. Get out of my office, right this instant!"

That was it, she had to get a response out of him. Mr. Jourdan looked up slowly as Petunia broke open the door. His eyes were cold and steady, "Quite an entry, but no. I have all the rights to remain silent." Petunia stood in the doorway, with a strong sense of authority in her voice.

"Listen up, Mr. Jourdan. You can play tough all you want, but I'll find out what I need to know, one way or another. The longer you resist, the harder it'll be on you. Your choice." Petunia left briefly and returned with her most trusted team she had known for more than ten years- Aisha, Hiroshi, Zain and Sophia. They arrested Mr. Jourdan swiftly and took him to the interrogation room without a word. Jourdan didn't care. He thought he could bribe the officials and get away with it.

In the interrogation room, Petunia and her team surrounded Mr. Jourdan, who sat silently, his expression unreadable. She demanded a response, "Mr. Jourdan, you have one last chance to cooperate. We know more than you think. And this time, I'll ensure you don't bribe our team. Start talking now, or we'll have to take this to another level." He hesitated for a bit and refused to speak again. This was getting irritating now. They had to use a narco analysis test with sodium pentothal to uncover the truth.

They prepared the truth serum and injected it into Jourdan's arm. He was tied up and thus, couldn't resist. Reluctantly, Mr. Jourdan began to speak, revealing a past filled with illicit activities—smuggling illegal substances and banned chemicals into the country—but nothing that tied him directly to the current incident. Nonetheless, they arrested him on non-bailable charges and he was given a life sentence in prison. Petunia was glad that she had potentially saved people from harmful substances but the trauma of Noa's death stayed with her. She had witnessed many cases in her lifetime, but none as distressing as this one.

She had to move on to the next person, Jordyn Taylor. Upon investigation, she found that Jordyn had been working as a scientist in Suncham for the welfare of the underprivileged communities. She originally hailed from Litnich and was yearning to make a change in the neighboring under-developed countries including her own. She had a clean record, nothing suspicious. Petunia was glad to have another suspect crossed off the list.

## CHAPTER 3

# THE CASE OF JORDYNN PARKER

Their last suspect was Mr. Jordynn Parker. He had a dark past, perhaps even darker than Jourdan Blake. No one knew his exact location, but whispers claimed he had an underground bunker on the outskirts of Furors, where he performed bizarre experiments. According to the *Times Furors* newspaper, there were reports of him developing a new infection, although there were no indications he planned to test it on anyone, given its hazardous potential. Yet now, with all the recent developments, Jordynn had become the prime suspect—and he had to be found.

Petunia and her crew arrived at the Furors-Beligia border, where he had allegedly been hiding for the last four years. For miles and miles, there was nothing but a vast, arid desert. It stretched before them like an endless sea of shimmering gold, each dune rising and falling like the waves of an unforgiving ocean. The air was thick, oppressive with heat. The sun hung high in the sky, baking the land below.

The bunker could be hidden anywhere beneath the heaps of sand. The thought sent a shiver down Petunia's spine, despite the heat. They had to start searching—but with extreme caution. The desert posed severe threats: dehydration, venomous wildlife, and natural disasters. They couldn't afford any mistakes. Petunia quickly gave orders, and the four team members split up, each assigned to search a one-kilometre radius. The desert stretched endlessly, and after hours of searching, nothing appeared to be out of the ordinary.

Sophia's voice crackled over the radio. She sounded drained, "Nothing here, Petunia. Moving forward."

Sophia had always been the quiet strength of the team. She had a steadfast calm even in the most dangerous situations. Petunia could hear the fatigue in her voice—this desert, this mission, it was pushing them all to their limits.

Petunia communicated with the rest of her crew. Zain, with his firm demeanor and analytical mind, was always the first to point out details others missed. He seemed focused as ever, but even his usual energy had been sapped by the relentless heat.

Then there was Hiroshi, always a bit of a wildcard, driven by his passion for discovery and a fondness for risk-taking. Normally, he'd be the one cracking jokes to keep spirits high, but today, he was silent. Despite his usual bravado, Petunia could sense the tension in him—this wasn't the time for humour, and even Hiroshi knew it.

Aisha, the heart of the team, was a natural empath, always checking in on others and keeping morale steady. Today, though, she seemed distant, likely conserving her energy for the gruelling trek ahead.

Petunia herself was feeling the pressure too, but she had to keep it together. Each member of her team had their own unique strength, and she relied on all of them, comforting them and motivating them over radio.

After walking nearly five kilometres in the blistering heat, Hiroshi communicated, "I've got something here. Feels solid, like it's buried."

The team rushed to his location and dug through the hot sand. Soon, the entrance to an underground bunker appeared before them. It was sealed tight. They all worked together, pouring their efforts into opening the heavy door. When it finally gave away, they were met with nothing but silence and the strong smell of decay. The place had been abandoned for who knew how long. Spiderwebs clung to every corner. Petunia's skin crawled at the thought of the venomous creatures that might be lurking.

But they had no choice—they had to go in. They put on their protective gear and descended into the bunker. The moment they stepped inside, a strong odour of chlorine gas hit them. It was overpowering, stinging their eyes and throats. They covered their mouths and noses with handkerchiefs, but Sophia, ever observant, was already showing signs of exposure. Red rashes bloomed across her skin, and a fine sheen of sweat appeared on her forehead.

"Sophia, you good?" Zain's voice was tight with concern.

"I'm fine," she replied, but there was a slight tremor to her voice.

They had to move quickly. Every second inside this bunker could be dangerous. The team searched the cramped space, but found little more than a few discarded test tubes and stains on the ground. Jordynn Parker was nowhere to be found. There were no real clues, just remnants of what might have been a trap.

"This is nothing but a distraction," Petunia muttered, frustration in her voice. She wanted to believe Jordynn was just leading them in circles, but something kept gnawing at her. What if they were walking straight into his twisted plan?

When they finally emerged from the bunker, relief washed over them as they breathed the fresh, though scorching air in. But Sophia was struggling. The red rashes on her skin had spread, and her breathing rate increased significantly. She tried to keep up a brave front, but Petunia could see the toll the chlorine exposure had taken on her.

Despite their concern, they had to keep moving. The desert was harsh, pressing down on them with an almost unbearable heat. Sophia's pace slowed, but she kept going, not wanting to be a burden. Petunia found herself glancing at her more often. She was concerned for her health. Sophia had always been the steady one, the one who held the team together even in tough times. Seeing her like this was worrying.

Suddenly, in the distance, an alarm began to blare—a deafening, grating sound that broke the desert silence. Without hesitation, Petunia told the team to follow it. They moved ahead quickly.

As they pushed on, Sophia stumbled. Zain quickly moved to her side; his expression nervous. "Let me help," he said calmly.

Sophia gave him a grateful, tired smile. "Thanks, Zain." His supportive presence and quiet encouragement created a moment of tranquility amid the harsh desert. This simple gesture of support made their tough journey feel a bit more bearable.

As they continued walking, the alarm noise grew louder, guiding them through the desert. The sun was brutal, and every step felt heavy. Petunia was getting more anxious; the alarm could mean they were close to Jordynn Parker or walking into another trap.

Sophia was exhausted, but Zain stayed close to help her. "We're almost there," he said, though he was worried. They kept moving, determined to find where the noise was coming from.

Eventually, they reached a bunch of old containers half-buried in the sand. The alarm noise was loudest from one of the containers. Petunia quickly opened the container door, and they saw an old, dusty radio system inside. It was clear now that the alarm was just a trick.

"This was a waste of time," Petunia said, frustrated.

Despite her struggle, Sophia spoke up. "We should look around for any hidden clues. Jordynn wouldn't just leave an alarm for no reason." The team spread out and searched the area around the containers.

After some time, as the sun began to set, Aisha found something. It was an old satellite dish, buried but still working.

"This could help us find Jordynn," Petunia said. "Let's see if it leads us to him."

They cleaned up the satellite dish and got it working. It began sending a signal pointing to a remote part of the desert. "This might be our best chance," Petunia said, feeling hopeful. "We need to follow this signal."

Zain nodded. "Let's do it," he said, determined.

As night fell, the team set off again, following the signal from the satellite dish. They were closer to finding Jordynn Parker and solving the mystery behind the alarms and traps.

As they followed the signal from the satellite dish, the desert night felt colder and more brutal. Exhausted but determined, the team reached an old, hidden facility buried in the sand. It looked abandoned, but Petunia felt something was wrong.

Inside, they found dusty equipment and photographs pinned to the wall. Some of the photos were recent and showed people they didn't recognize.

"This doesn't make sense," Petunia said, uneasy. "Who took these pictures?"

Hiroshi found a hidden door behind some crates. They opened it to reveal a room full of files and documents. As they sifted through the papers, a chilling truth emerged. Jordynn Parker had been working in this lab on dangerous infections, but he had been forced to develop stronger versions by Mastermind. Jordynn had refused to continue with the work, and for that, he was murdered.

Petunia found a letter sent by Mastermind that confirmed the fact that Jordynn's defiance had led to his death. Mastermind had manipulated him through threats and coercion just like he had done with Noa. When Jordynn finally refused to create any more dangerous infections, his punishment was brutal.

The team followed the clues and stumbled upon a freezer room; its door slightly ajar. Inside, they found Jordynn's body. He was drenched, his lifeless form lying in a pool of icy water. The harsh conditions of the freezer had turned his final moments into a grim scene. The room was stark and silent, with no signs of other people or activity.

Their hearts sank as they saw Jordynn's body. "He was left here to die," Sophia said softly. "They used this place to hide their tracks." Hiroshi agreed, "Indeed. He was a man trying to bring a change, perhaps reduce the intensity of this new disaster. Sad, he passed away." This entire case was getting concerning. Two lives gone, taken by Mastermind's cruelty. The team knew they had to do justice to both Noa and Jordynn and prevent him from taking more lives.

# CHAPTER 4

# ONE STEP CLOSER

The team, gathered in the cold, dimly lit room, feeling the weight of their mission pressing down on them. Petunia looked around at her team, her voice steady but filled with determination. "We need to stick together until we find out who's behind all of this. No matter how tough it gets, we'll face it together."

Zain nodded, "We're a team. We've come this far, and we're not stopping now."

Hiroshi and Aisha, both looking equally determined, joined in. "We'll get it done," Hiroshi said, a spark of determination in his eyes. "We're in this together."

Petunia picked up her radio and contacted the Furors Department. "We need a truck to transport Jordynn's body to the city for a proper burial, and we need to get Sophia to the hospital. She's becoming unconscious."

The department responded quickly, and soon a truck arrived. Zain stayed close to Sophia. As they prepared to load Jordynn's body and get Sophia the care she needed, Zain spoke softly to her. "You're doing great, Sophia. Just hang on, we'll get you to the hospital." Sophia smiled weakly at him, "Thank you for supporting me, mate. Appreciate it."

The team worked together to carefully place Jordynn's body in the truck. And as they drove toward the city, they stayed by Sophia's side in the truck.

After reaching the city, the team immediately rushed Sophia to the hospital. The moment the truck stopped, the medical staff at Furors Maple Hospital quickly wheeled her inside. Zain stayed close, his worry for her obvious, but he remained composed. Petunia, Hiroshi, and Aisha waited anxiously as doctors took Sophia into the emergency room for treatment.

The team stood together in the hospital hallway, exhausted but determined. Petunia glanced at Zain, who hadn't left Sophia's side since they had found Jordynn's bunker. "She's tough. She'll pull through," she said, trying to reassure both him and herself.

Zain nodded, but his gaze remained fixed on the door. "Yeah, that girl is stronger than she looks."

After ensuring that Sophia was in good hands, they turned their attention to the city morgue, where Jordynn's body had been transported. Though Jordynn had been a critical player in the creation of the infections, the team felt a sense of duty to ensure his body was handled with care. Despite his misdeeds, he had been a victim in the end, caught in the deadly web of Mastermind's plans.

At the morgue, the city coroner confirmed that Jordynn's death had been ruthless. The team stood silently as the coroner explained the details.

Petunia sighed deeply, "We need to get to the bottom of this, fast," she said, her voice low. "Jordynn's dead because he refused.

Someone's still out there, pushing this agenda."

Aisha nodded in agreement. "We're closer, but there's still too much we don't know."

As they prepared to leave the morgue, the team made a pact. They wouldn't rest until the mastermind was brought to justice.

The team left the morgue, more united than ever. They had solved one piece of the puzzle, but the bigger mystery remained— who was behind all of this? With Sophia recovering and Jordynn's death fresh on their minds, they set their sights on their next step: finding who Mastermind truly was.

They had crossed off every suspect on their list. Each lead, each theory, had unravelled into nothing. The Mastermind behind this chaos was none of them. Petunia stood with the list in hand, staring at the names they had gathered. Jordynn Parker was dead. The rest were either irrelevant or distractions. It felt like they had been chasing shadows all along.

A frustrating thought lingered in the back of her mind: what if the mastermind had never been directly connected to Jordane, Jordynn, or any of the suspects they'd considered? What if this entire case was one big red herring—a meticulously constructed deception to throw them off course?

"This makes it so much harder," Petunia muttered, crumpling the paper in her hand. The room was tense, the weight of uncertainty pressing on them all. Mastermind was still out there, hiding in the shadows, and now they were back at square one.

Zain leaned against the wall; his arms crossed. "So, we've been chasing ghosts?"

"Feels like it," Aisha replied, discontent evident in her voice. "Everything we thought we knew was just a diversion."

"But this isn't over." Petunia's voice was firm. "If he's still out there, he's going to make another move. He always does."

Hiroshi nodded, pacing the room. "We might need to wait for him to slip up. He's careful, but if we keep the pressure on, he's bound to make a mistake."

As the tension hung in the air, a message beeped through Petunia's phone. She glanced at it and she sighed in relief, "It's from the hospital. Sophia's stable, but the doctor says it'll be a while before she's fully recovered."

Zain's shoulders visibly relaxed. "At least she's safe now."

Petunia's eyes flickered toward Zain. "You should go check on her. She needs the rest, and we all need to be at full strength for whatever comes next."

Zain hesitated but nodded. "Yeah, I'll head over. Keep me updated."

As Zain left, the rest of the team gathered around the table. "We can't just sit around waiting," Aisha said, "There has to be something we're missing. Some clue or trail we overlooked."

Petunia nodded, her mind racing. "We'll go back through everything. Every report, every document, every name. No stone unturned. If the mastermind is out there, we'll find him."

The team split up, each taking a stack of case files to review. Hours passed in silence, interrupted only by the occasional rustle of paper or soft sigh of frustration. But the more they dug, the more it seemed like they were chasing a phantom. The mastermind had left no obvious traces—at least, none they could find.

As the team continued their deep dive into the case, Hiroshi's phone buzzed on the table, breaking the silence. He glanced at the screen, his brow furrowing in concern. "We've got a problem."

Aisha and Petunia looked up, tension already creeping into the air. "What is it?" Petunia asked.

Hiroshi's face was anxious as he read the message aloud. "The Furors government just issued an emergency warning. There's been an outbreak—people are getting sick all over the city. It's spreading fast, and the symptoms match the infection Mastermind was working on."

Petunia's heart sank. This was worse than she'd imagined. Mastermind hadn't just been hiding—he had already set his plan in motion. "An outbreak? How did it spread?"

"They don't know yet," Hiroshi replied, scrolling through the message. "But the government is locking down parts of the city. Hospitals are overwhelmed."

Aisha leaned forward, her voice urgent. "This can't be a coincidence. The infection Mastermind worked on—it's been released. We're too late."

Petunia's mind raced, piecing together the puzzle. If the infection was out, that meant Mastermind had found a way to weaponize it. The fire at the warehouse, Jordynn's murder, all of it had been leading to this moment. But how did the infection get out? Was it airborne? Waterborne? They had no way of knowing yet.

"We need to act fast," Petunia said, her voice tight with worry. "If the infection is spreading, we need to find out where it started and how to contain it before it gets worse."

Hiroshi exclaimed, "The Furors government wouldn't issue a warning unless things were already out of control. We have to contact them directly and get more details."

Petunia nodded. "Do it. We need to know the scale of this. If we don't act now, this could turn into a full-blown epidemic."

As Hiroshi dialled into the government's emergency line, Petunia turned to Aisha.

"We need to figure out how the infection was released. There's no way this is random. Mastermind had to have a plan, and there's a good chance we're going to find a pattern in where the infection is spreading first."

Aisha was already scanning her tablet, pulling up the city's outbreak map. "Look here," she said, pointing to the screen. "The first few cases are clustered around the eastern district—near that underground biotech lab where we found all those people trapped."

Hiroshi put the call on hold and concluded, "If the infection came from there, it means Mastermind could've possibly entered it to extract whatever was left of it."

Aisha sighed, "But that facility was burnt out, and we cleared it. How could the infection still come from there?"

Petunia's eyes narrowed. "What if there's more? A second level, even deeper underground, that we missed? Mastermind obviously knew about it, he could've accessed it. Maybe, that part of the lab never burnt down."

Aisha zoomed in on the map, focusing on the lab's location. "Yes! If there was a hidden section deeper underground, it could've housed more samples or research material. It's possible that Mastermind reactivated something after the fire."

Just then, Hiroshi, still on the line with government officials, held up a hand to get their attention. "They've confirmed something. The first few cases were traced back to a delivery service that operated close to that lab. One of the workers unknowingly got infected and spread it during their rounds more than a week ago."

Petunia's heart sank. "So, the infection wasn't just released recently—it's been circulating for quite some time."

Aisha bit her lip. "That means we're already behind. Mastermind's been ahead of us the whole time."

Hiroshi hung up, his expression serious. "The government's locking down the eastern district. They've got teams on the ground, but they need more information before they can contain it. They've asked us to keep investigating—we're their best shot."

Petunia nodded. "We have to first scrutinize the lab and question the delivery worker. If there's another level underground, that's where we'll find our answers. I'll call Zain and Sophia to see if they can tag along."

# CHAPTER 5

# GONE

Petunia dialled Zain and Sophia, her voice steady despite the urgency of the situation. Zain answered quickly, "Petunia, what's going on?"

"We're going back to the lab," Petunia explained. "There's a chance there's another level underground. We need to check it out and question a delivery worker. How's Sophia feeling? Can you guys meet us there?"

"Understood. Sophia is doing much better now, quite a tough girl. We'll be there as soon as possible," Zain replied. The call ended, and Petunia turned to her team, determination in her eyes.

By the time they arrived at the lab, Zain and Sophia were already waiting. The lab was cordoned off, security still on high alert. Petunia flashed her badge to the officers on duty. "We need to get inside. There's new evidence we need to investigate."

The officers let them through, and they made their way into the lab. The place was eerily quiet, the atmosphere tense. Petunia led the team to the area where the delivery worker, Gregor, had left the package.

"Let's start by examining the area," Petunia instructed. "If there's another level, it should be hidden but accessible." The whole place was burnt down, ashes and rusting metal parts everywhere with melted equipment all over the floor.

As they searched, Aisha noticed something unusual. "Look here," she said, pointing to a section of the wall that seemed slightly out of place. "This wall doesn't match the rest."

Petunia examined the wall closely. It was a false panel, a hidden door disguised to blend in with the surroundings. "Good eye, Aisha," Petunia said, pulling at the panel. It creaked open, revealing a narrow staircase leading down.

They descended cautiously into the dimly lit underground chamber. The air was cool but dusty. The space was cluttered with old equipment and stacks of papers. It was clear this area had been used recently.

"Spread out and search for anything unusual," Petunia ordered. The team fanned out, their flashlights cutting through the darkness.

Zain was the first to find something significant. Behind a stack of crates, he uncovered a large, heavy door. "Petunia, come here. I think we found something."

Petunia joined Zain and examined the door. It was locked but seemed to have been recently used. With a little effort, they managed to pry it open, revealing a small room filled with vials and test tubes. It was a hidden laboratory, untouched but clearly operational.

"This must be where they were working on the infection," Petunia said, her voice filled with awe. "We need to gather as much evidence as we can."

The team worked quickly, collecting samples and documents. They found detailed notes on infection strains, experiments, and a list of contacts. The more they uncovered, the more they realized the scope of the mastermind's operation.

Suddenly, Hiroshi's phone rang. He looked at the screen and scowled. "It's the Furors government. They have another update."

Petunia took the call, her heart racing. "What's the news?"

"There's been another outbreak in the city centre," the official said, voice tense. "It's spreading rapidly. We need to contain it immediately."

Petunia's mind raced. Mastermind was taking his plan to the next level. They needed to act fast. "We're on it. We'll be in touch."

As they packed up their findings, Petunia felt the weight of their mission bearing down heavily. They had evidence, but it was clear Mastermind's plans were far from over. The city was in danger, and time was running out.

The team exited the underground chamber and they decided to question the delivery worker next.

At the delivery company's hub, chaos greeted them. The delivery worker they needed to question, Gregor, had been quarantined, his condition deteriorating quickly. A young security guard led them to him. "He's bad," the guard warned. "But he might be able to talk."

Petunia and the others approached the makeshift quarantine room, where Gregor lay weakly, his breathing laboured and his skin pale. His eyes flickered open as they drew near.

"Gregor," Petunia began softly. "We need to know about the lab. The package you delivered—who gave it to you?"

Gregor coughed violently before rasping, "I didn't know... I was just doing my job. A woman gave me a package... told me to leave it in a specific spot near the lab."

Petunia froze. "A woman?"

Gregor nodded weakly. "Yeah... she was careful. Wore a mask, gloves... everything. I never saw her face."

"A woman?!" Zain repeated, the revelation hitting him hard. "Are you sure?"

Gregor coughed again, each breath sounding more painful. "Yes... she was in charge. Told me... it was just the beginning."

Petunia's pulse quickened. A woman. All this time, they'd been chasing after shadows, assuming Mastermind was a man. But it had been her. She had been pulling the strings all along.

Just then, Hiroshi's phone buzzed sharply in the quiet room. He read the alert and said, "There's been another outbreak."

Petunia's heart dropped. "Where?"

Hiroshi looked up, eyes wide. "The city's main hospital. The infection is spreading faster than they've ever seen."

Petunia exchanged a look with Zain, Sophia and Aisha. The mastermind wasn't just planning her next move—she was already executing it.

They turned to leave but just as they stepped away, Gregor muttered something, his voice barely audible.

Petunia leaned closer, catching his words as he drifted into unconsciousness.

"The mask... the woman said... it's only about to get worse."

The room fell silent, his words slowly sinking in. Petunia stood frozen, a chill running down her spine.

Gregor's enigmatic warning frightened them. The city's main hospital was already overwhelmed, and now it seemed like Mastermind was planning something even more sinister.

"We need to figure out what 'the mask' means," Petunia said, her voice steady despite the rising panic. "It could be a code or a clue to her next move."

Hiroshi, still on the phone with the Furors government, provided an update. "They're reporting an unusual pattern in the infection's spread. It's not following any natural outbreak model—they think it's being deliberately manipulated."

Petunia's mind raced. The mastermind wasn't just spreading an infection; she was composing it like a puppet master. The city was in a state of emergency, and the clues were becoming increasingly urgent.

"Let's split up," Petunia decided. "Hiroshi, Aisha, you two go to the hospital and see if you can get any information on the infection's behaviour. Zain, Sophia, and I will see if we can find out more about this woman he mentioned."

In the dimly lit lab, they worked quickly, digging into Mastermind's files and records. They discovered that she had been working on a project related to the infection, but her notes were fragmented and cryptic. Amidst the chaos of the files, they found a partially burned document with the word "MASK" written prominently.

"This must be it," Sophia said, pointing to the document. "The mask could be a reference to something Mastermind is using to hide her identity."

Sophia kept a sharp eye out for any additional clues. "Look at this," she said, holding up a faded map with markings around several key locations. "It seems like Mastermind has targeted specific areas. These places might be significant."

Petunia nodded, taking the map and studying the locations. "These areas have a large population of immigrants, her main targets. If she's planning something, this might be where she's going to execute it."

Meanwhile, Hiroshi and Aisha were at the hospital, navigating through the chaotic patients and medical staff. They spoke with doctors and reviewed data on the infection's spread. The infection's rapid and unpredictable spread confirmed the government's fears.

"This is beyond anything we've seen," a hospital administrator told them. "The infection appears to be evolving. It's as if it's learning to bypass our defenses."

Aisha frowned. "This doesn't sound like a natural mutation. It's almost like someone is controlling its behaviour."

Hiroshi nodded. "We need to get this information back to Petunia and the team. They need to know how severe the situation is."

Back at the lab, Petunia, Zain, and Sophia continued their search. They found a file marked "CONFIDENTIAL," hidden in a drawer. Inside, there were detailed schematics for a new type of mask—one that appeared to be designed to protect against the infection but also had other, unknown functions.

"This mask could be the key," Petunia said, her voice tense with realization. "If it's designed to protect against the infection, it means Mastermind is planning something big. She wants to control how the infection spreads and how people react to it."

As they gathered their findings, the Furors port reported a new development—a mysterious shipment of masks arriving at one of the high-traffic areas marked on the map.

"We need to stop that shipment," Petunia said urgently. "If the mastermind is using those masks, we need to intercept them before it's too late."

The team raced to the location, their hearts pounding. The city was on edge, and every second mattered.

As they approached the delivery point, Petunia's phone buzzed urgently. She answered, her voice barely concealing her rising anxiety. It was Milly, her roommate, but the distress in her voice made Petunia's heart race.

"Petunia, it's Diana. She's missing."

Petunia's breath caught. "What? What do you mean?"

"There was a note," Milly explained, her voice cracking. "It says, 'Your daughter will only be returned when the city's chaos reaches its peak. Stop the delivery, and you can say good-bye, forever."

# MASTERMIND

# Chapter 1

# Disaster Unfolds

Petunia's heart pounded as she hung up the phone, Milly's words pressing heavily on her chest. Her daughter, Diana, was missing, and the note left behind was a chilling threat. Her mind was racing to connect the dots.

"Your daughter will only be returned when the city's chaos reaches its peak. Stop the delivery, and you can say good-bye, forever."

The message was clear: Mastermind had taken Diana as a part of her plan, using her as leverage to manipulate Petunia and disrupt the investigation.

Petunia took a deep breath, trying to steady herself. She turned to her team, who had been watching her with concern. "I have to go. Diana's been kidnapped, and I need to find her. You need to keep pursuing Mastermind. I trust you all to handle this."

Zain, Sophia, Hiroshi, and Aisha exchanged worried glances but nodded in understanding. "We'll find her, Petunia," Sophia said, placing a reassuring hand on her shoulder. "You stay safe and focus on getting Diana back."

Petunia's heart raced as she reached the lab and pushed through its entrance, her mind focused on one desperate goal: finding her daughter, Diana. The lab, usually a hub of scientific activity, now felt ominously quiet. She knew the lab was a safe retreat for Mastermind and she could've hidden her there.

She sprinted down the narrow hallways, calling out for Diana, her voice echoing off the sterile walls. "Diana! Where are you?" The silence that followed each shout was deafening. She checked every room and corridor, but there was no sign of her daughter.

The lab had a labyrinthine layout, and as Petunia moved deeper, her hope began to wane. Just when she was about to give in to despair, she heard a faint sound—almost like a whimper—coming from a closed door. Her heart leapt.

Petunia reached the door and hesitated, her hand trembling as she grasped the handle. She took a deep breath and opened it. There, slumped against the wall, was Diana. Her daughter's pale face and laboured breathing were a sight that tore at Petunia's heart.

"Diana!" Petunia's voice cracked with emotion as she rushed to her side. Diana looked up weakly, her eyes glassy but filled with relief. "Mom... don't come close...," she whispered, barely able to speak.

Petunia looked at her weak form from a distance, concerned. "We need to get you out of here," she said gently, her voice calm despite the fear that gripped her. Petunia reached for her phone, dialling for immediate medical assistance. Her words conveyed the gravity of the situation.

The medical team arrived soon and quickly assessed Diana's condition. Petunia felt a pang of dread as she watched them work.

She knew she couldn't afford to stay in the lab; the infection was too dangerous, and her own safety was at risk.

Petunia carefully handed Diana over to the medics, her heart aching at the sight of her daughter being taken away. Diana was transported to a secure treatment area.

Petunia's heart thumped as she considered the situation. Mastermind's actions were beyond anything they had anticipated. Kidnapping Diana, only to let Petunia easily find her infected, was deeply worrying. It was almost as if Mastermind was playing a twisted game, testing Petunia's patience. How did she know Petunia? Was she connected to her in any way? Had they met before?

Petunia quickly made her way back to the team, her mind still racing with bizarre thoughts. The situation surrounding Diana's kidnapping was hard on her, but she knew she couldn't afford to lose focus now.

Arriving at the shipment area, she saw an enigmatic woman, now restrained in handcuffs, being led away by her team. Her black outfit blended into the shadows, while her mask concealed her true identity.

Her character radiated an eerie calmness. Petunia's gaze followed her, noting the slight tension in her movements as they escorted her out.

Petunia approached the team, her face set with determination. "What do we know?" she asked, her voice pressing.

Hiroshi informed, "We caught her near the shipment area. She was acting suspicious, and her outfit matches some descriptions we've seen before. But she hasn't given us much information."

Petunia's eyes narrowed. "She's either Mastermind or someone who knows a lot. We need to interrogate her and find out what she knows."

The team moved quickly to a secure room where they could question the woman. She sat calmly, her eyes betraying a hint of anxiety. As the interrogation began, it became clear that she wasn't talking easily. They took off her mask. She wasn't a lady they recognised.

Aisha took the lead, her tone firm but calm. "We know you're connected to the mastermind. You've been caught in the act. Tell us what you know."

The woman remained silent for a moment before speaking. "I'm just a messenger," she said quietly, glancing around nervously. "My role was to make sure the infection reached immigrant populations and to create distractions."

Petunia's heart pounded. Why? What did Mastermind hope to achieve with this horrific act? The woman's next words only deepened the mystery. "The masks are meant only for Mastermind's family so they can protect themselves."

Petunia's mind raced. A family? Mastermind has a family?! This new twist was unsettling. The woman's face was pale, her hands shaking as she continued. "I'm really scared of the authorities," she admitted, her voice trembling. "I wasn't supposed to say anything. I... I never wanted to do this. Mastermind forced me to, taking hostage of my only son." She started to weep. Petunia said, "It's alright. This is a safe space. Tell us what you know and we promise to get your son back to safety." She responded, "Um... alright... I'll tell you what I know. Mastermind isn't just trying to spread the infection. She's creating fear and confusion."

Petunia leaned in, "Tell us more. What else do you know?"

The woman swallowed hard, her voice trembling. "The mastermind planned this in stages. She spread the infection in certain areas to make people sick and create panic. But it's not just about the infection. She wants to control everything, make people so scared that they'll accept extreme measures.

She targets immigrants because she thinks they're more vulnerable and less protected. By causing trouble in their communities, she hopes to disrupt the city and use the chaos to push her own agenda. It's all part of her plan to take control and manipulate the situation."

Her fear was evident, but she kept talking. "I don't know much but...um...there are key locations where the infection was distributed. I can help you find them. But you have to act fast. She's prepared for every possible outcome."

The team moved quickly, taking the woman's information seriously. The woman was arrested and taken into custody, but her revelations had given them a crucial lead.

They now had specific locations to investigate, and time was of the essence.

The team split up. Petunia and Aisha headed for the eastern district, where the infection had first appeared. The streets were eerily quiet, the usual bustle replaced by a palpable tension. They knew that they were racing against time to prevent further outbreaks.

As they arrived at one of the key sites, Petunia felt a sense of dread. The building they were investigating was a small warehouse with minimal security, seemingly abandoned. They entered cautiously, their footsteps echoing in the emptiness. Petunia's flashlight beam cut through the darkness, revealing discarded crates and forgotten equipment.

In the dim light, Petunia noticed something unusual: a series of symbols scratched into the walls. They seemed random at first, but as she studied them, a pattern began to emerge. It looked like a code, possibly indicating the locations where the infection had been distributed. She quickly took photos and made notes, hoping to decipher the code later.

Aisha's voice interrupted her thoughts. "Petunia, over here!" She called from the back of the warehouse. Petunia hurried to her side, where she was examining a large, sealed container. The label on the container read "Quarantine Use Only." Aisha pried it open, revealing vials of a substance that looked alarmingly similar to the infection they had been tracking.

"This has to be part of Mastermind's plan," Petunia said, "We need to get this back to the lab for analysis. It might give us more clues about the next stages of her plan."

Meanwhile, Zain, Sophia and Hiroshi were working tirelessly at central command, piecing together the information they had gathered. Zain was analysing the spread of the infection, while Hiroshi coordinated with emergency services to manage the crisis. The situation was dire, with hospitals overflowing and the city on high alert.

Sophia's screen lit up with a new development. "Petunia, you need to see this," she called her, "The infection has spread to a new area. It's affecting a community in the western district. It's likely that Mastermind is using this location to expand her agenda."

Petunia and Aisha rushed to the new site, arriving to find chaos unfolding. The community, once a place of refuge and support, was now a hotbed of infection. People were panicking, trying to escape the infection that seemed to have taken hold rapidly. This was worse than the bubonic plague.

Petunia worked with local officials to establish a quarantine zone, ensuring that the infected were contained and treated.

Back at the lab, the vials from the warehouse were analysed, revealing a disturbing truth. The infection was indeed more potent than before, and it had been modified to spread more easily. Mastermind's plan was evolving, and they had to adapt quickly.

Petunia's phone rang. The caller ID showed it was from the jail. She answered, her heart pounding.

"Ms. Petunia, we have a situation," the guard's voice was shaky. "The woman... she escaped."

Petunia froze. "What do you mean she escaped?"

"She left a note. It reads, 'Try and stop me. I'm not what I look like. I was the Mastermind. My face wasn't real, you fools—catch me if you can. Hahaha!'"

Petunia's blood ran cold as the words sank in. She called Zain, Sophia and Hiroshi to arrive at their location. She informed them of the news.

Petunia slammed the phone down and looked at her team. "She's gone. It was her all along. The woman we arrested... She was Mastermind."

Zain's eyes widened. "The one we just had in custody?"

Petunia nodded, a bitter feeling welling up in her chest. "She fooled us. She wore a wax mask the whole time, pretending to be someone else."

Hiroshi frowned. "So what now? How do we find her?"

"We need to figure out her next move," Petunia said, forcing herself to think clearly. "She's not done yet. That note was a challenge. She's daring us to try and stop her."

# Chapter 2

# The Game Is On

Aisha pulled up a map of the infection spread on her tablet. "We know her targets were immigrant communities. She wanted to create chaos, make them vulnerable, and break the city apart. But why? What's her ultimate goal?"

Petunia sighed. "It's all about control. She's stirring panic to step in and manipulate everything. The more chaos she causes, the more desperate people become. She'll use that desperation to push her agenda, maybe even start a biological war. She's been testing infections on the most vulnerable aka the immigrants, and now she's spreading the strongest one. We need to stop her before this escalates and panic ensues in our entire continent."

Hiroshi, still shaken by the woman's escape, added, "We know she's targeted key locations across the city. We need to hit those fast before she can carry out the next phase of her plan."

The team distributed the locations, preparing to investigate them as quickly as possible. There was no time to lose.

For Petunia, the fight had become personal. The mastermind had infected her daughter, Diana. But why? Was it just to send a message or to break her spirit? Either way, Petunia wasn't going to let this criminal slip away again. She was fuelled by anger and fear, a dangerous combination that sharpened her focus.

As they rushed towards their assigned locations, the tension within the team grew. Mastermind had dodged them once, but they couldn't afford to fall behind again.

While examining one of the suspected infection distribution sites, Zain's phone buzzed. He glanced down and froze. "Petunia, we've got another problem," he said, showing her the screen.

Her heart skipped a beat. "What now?!"

Zain turned the phone toward her, a live broadcast blinking on the screen. "It's from Mastermind. She's addressing the entire city."

Petunia's stomach twisted. "She's making her move."

Sophia quickly tapped into the broadcast, Mastermind's distorted voice ringing across the room.

"I hope you're all watching closely," Mastermind said, her tone laced with menace. "This city belongs to me now. Your leaders are powerless. The infection is spreading, and there's nothing you can do to stop it. This is only the beginning."

The broadcast cut off, but the damage was done. The streets erupted in panic, just as the mastermind had intended. Chaos was spreading faster than the infection itself.

"We need to shut this down," Aisha said, typing furiously on her tablet. "If people keep watching, it'll create more fear and disorder."

Petunia's jaw tightened. "We can't let her control Furors. Find her. She can't be far."

But just as she issued the order, another message flashed on her phone—this time, it was personal.

"You couldn't save your daughter from being infected, Petunia. How do you expect to save an entire city?"

Petunia's fists tightened. The mastermind wasn't just taunting the city; she was taunting her. This wasn't a random criminal. This was someone with intimate knowledge of their lives—someone powerful, manipulative, and far more dangerous than they had thought before.

"Enough games," Petunia murmured. "We need to lure her out. If she's this confident, we can use that against her."

Zain frowned. "How do we do that?"

"We make her think she's winning," Petunia replied, her voice steady. "We set a trap, leaking false information that the infection is spreading uncontrollably in a specific area. If she's watching, she'll take the bait and try to capitalize on it."

The team exchanged glances. It was risky, but they didn't have much of a choice.

Petunia's plan could be their best shot at turning the tables.

They moved quickly, carefully planting fake reports and broadcasting them through various channels. The trap was set. Now, all they could do was wait.

Hours passed. The city's unrest continued to grow, but the team kept their eyes on the screens, waiting for any sign that Mastermind had taken the bait.

Suddenly, a notification popped up on Aisha's screen. "Got her," she whispered, her eyes lighting up. "She's moving toward the area we flagged. She thinks the infection is out of control there."

Petunia stood, her determination revived. "Good. Let's end this."

The team geared up, adrenaline surging through their veins. This was their chance to catch Mastermind before she could wreak more havoc. The next few hours were critical and would determine the city's fate.

As they moved swiftly toward the targeted location, the streets were in disarray, reflecting the terror and confusion Mastermind had spread. Petunia's thoughts drifted to Diana, still fighting the infection, as she pushed forward. There was no turning back now.

They arrived at the point where Mastermind was expected to appear. The area was strangely quiet, the tension in the air intense. They hid, waiting for the right moment to strike.

Minutes felt like hours as they lay in wait. Then, through the shadows, a figure emerged. She wore the same black outfit from before with a mask hiding her identity. Suddenly, she seemed familiar...

# CHAPTER 3

# ANTIDOTE

**Z**ain clenched his jaw, eyes locked on the figure stepping out into the open. "Is that her?" "It has to be," Petunia whispered, her pulse quickening.

Mastermind moved carefully, completely unaware that she was walking right into their trap. Petunia gave the signal, her heart pounding in her chest. "Now."

The team moved quickly, surrounding her, cutting off any escape route. But something wasn't right. Mastermind's calmness never wavered, as if she knew what was coming, as if this was all part of her sick plan.

Hiroshi stepped forward, his voice steady. "It's over. You're surrounded."

Mastermind raised her hands slowly, a smirk tugging at the corner of her lips. "Is it really over?" she said, mockingly.

Petunia's eyes narrowed. "You've got nowhere to run."

"Run?" Mastermind tilted her head slightly, her eyes glinting with something sinister. "Oh, Petunia... you still don't get it, do you?"

Petunia's heart skipped a beat, an uneasy feeling settling in her stomach. Something was off. Mastermind was too calm, too confident.

Then, suddenly, the sound of footsteps echoed from behind them. Petunia spun around, her heart racing. A group of masked figures emerged from the shadows, closing in on the team. They were armed, moving with precision.

"They were waiting for us," Sophia muttered, her hand reaching for her weapon.

Mastermind smiled wider now, watching as her backup cornered the team. "Did you really think you'd catch me that easily? I've been watching you all along."

The pressure skyrocketed. Petunia glanced at Zain, who nodded, ready to fight their way out. But before the team could make a move, Mastermind raised a small device in her hand, pressing a button. Instantly, a series of explosions erupted in the distance.

Petunia's stomach dropped. The infection distribution points. The chaos was already beginning. "Do you hear that?" Mastermind whispered, leaning forward with a chilling grin. "That's the sound of your failure. The city is mine now." Petunia clenched her fists, trying to steady her breath. "We're not done yet."

"Oh, but you are." The mastermind's eyes gleamed with victory. "You see, this was never about escaping. It was about leading you right where I wanted."

Petunia's mind raced. They had been so focused on capturing her, they hadn't seen the bigger picture. Mastermind had lured them into a trap, distracting them while her real plan unfolded.

But then, just as quickly, the masked figures surrounding them began to fall back, one by one. Mastermind's smirk faltered as confusion flashed across her face.

Zain stepped forward. "You're not the only one who can set traps."

Petunia smiled grimly. "We knew you'd try something like this. So, we set up a little surprise of our own."

Mastermind's backup was being taken down by reinforcements, agents Petunia had called in earlier, just in case. The tide had turned, and now, it was Mastermind who was trapped.

For the first time, a hint of terror crossed her face. She tried to step back, but it was too late. Petunia moved in, grabbing her by the arm, her voice firm. "It's over. You're coming with us."

But as Petunia dragged her toward the waiting van, something clicked in her mind. Mastermind's face... It was familiar. Too familiar.

Petunia's breath caught in her throat. She yanked the woman's mask off, revealing the face underneath.

It was Levana.

"No..." Petunia whispered, her heart pounding in her chest. "It can't be."

Levana, Noa's wife—the grieving widow they had met at the beginning of this nightmare—was Mastermind.

Petunia's mind raced. Levana had been right in front of them, playing the part of the devastated wife, pretending to know nothing. She had fooled everyone, including her own family. Her kids, her friends—none of them knew her true identity.

Levana smirked, seeing the horror on Petunia's face. "Surprised?" she asked, her voice dripping with satisfaction. "You should have seen this coming."

Petunia felt sick. Levana had set up everything—the infection, the chaos, the murders. She had even killed her own husband, all to push forward her twisted plan.

"Why?" Petunia asked, her voice shaking with disbelief. "Why kill your own husband? Why all of this?"

Levana's smile was cold, her eyes devoid of emotion, a true psychopath, "Noa was a fool. He was weak, standing in my way. I had to get rid of him. And as for the rest of it... It's all about power. Control! This city will bend to my will, and I'll be the one pulling the strings."

Petunia's stomach churned. Levana had sacrificed everything for her horrid agenda, even the people closest to her.

"You won't get away with this," Petunia said, her voice hardening. "We're going to stop you."

Levana chuckled, her eyes gleaming with malice. "Oh, Petunia... you still don't understand, do you? This is just the beginning. I've already set things in motion that you can't stop."

Just then, Petunia's phone buzzed. She glanced down, her heart throbbing as she saw the message flash across the screen: *Outbreak confirmed. Multiple locations.*

Levana's laugh echoed in the cold night air. "See? You're already too late."

Petunia stared at her with a dangerous look in her eyes. They had captured Levana, but her plan was still unfolding. The city was wobbling on the edge of chaos.

As Levana was taken into custody, Petunia knew this was far from over. The real fight had just begun.

And as she watched Levana being taken away, Petunia couldn't shake the feeling that the worst was yet to come.

# Chapter 4

# The End?

The heavy steel door of the interrogation room slammed shut, the echo lingering in the still air. Levana sat peacefully in the centre, her wrists bound to the table by chains that rattled with each movement. The overhead light cast a shadow across her face, however she remained unflustered. Petunia stood on the other side of the two-way mirror, staring at the woman who had torn apart her city.

"Are you sure you want to do this?" Hiroshi asked, his voice barely more than a whisper. He knew what was at stake—Petunia wasn't just facing a criminal mastermind. She was confronting the woman who had endangered her daughter's life.

Petunia didn't answer. She took a breath and entered the room, shutting the door behind her. The air inside felt suffocating. Levana, however, looked up with a cold grin.

"Petunia. You look tired. Have you not been sleeping well?" Her voice was smooth, venomous, designed to pierce through any armour Petunia had left.

Petunia's jaw tightened. She wouldn't give Levana the satisfaction. "You're going to tell me where the antidote is."

Levana raised an eyebrow, amused. "Is that how you want to start this conversation? I thought you'd want to talk about your dear daughter, Diana."

An expression of pain crossed Petunia's face, but she quickly hid it to appear strong. Diana's condition had worsened over the past few hours. The infection—crafted so meticulously by Levana—was unlike anything they had ever seen. There was no cure, no known treatment. And the only person who held the antidote was sitting right in front of her.

"Where is it?" Petunia demanded, her voice low and dangerous.

Levana leaned back in her chair, as though she were the one in control. "You really think I'll just hand it over?"

Petunia slammed her hands down on the table, the metal rattling under her force. "I swear, if anything happens to my daughter and the people—"

"You'll what?" Levana interrupted, her eyes gleaming with malice. "Kill me? Torture me? It doesn't matter, Petunia. I've already won. Your people are casualties of war, nothing more."

Petunia's chest heaved with rage, but she forced herself to remain calm. Levana wanted her to lose control. She wanted Petunia to fall apart, and Petunia wouldn't give her that.

"Tell me where the antidote is," Petunia said. "Or I will make sure you never see daylight again."

Levana's smile faded for the briefest moment. For the first time, Petunia saw a flicker of uncertainty in her eyes. "You don't scare me."

Petunia leaned in, her voice a whisper. "I don't need to scare you. But I can make your life a living hell. You'll rot in a cell, forgotten, while I tear apart every piece of your operation. I'll dismantle everything you've built, piece by piece."

Levana's eyes narrowed. "You think you can stop it? The infection is already spreading, and you have no idea how far it's gone."

"I don't care about your infection right now," Petunia hissed, her patience thinning. "I care about my city. Where. Is. The. Antidote."

For a long moment, the two women stared at each other in silence, the tension thick enough to cut with a knife. Levana's smirk slowly returned, but this time it was more cautious, more controlled.

"Fine," Levana said at last. "I'll tell you where it is. But you won't like the price."

Petunia's heart pounded in her chest, but she kept her face neutral. "What do you want?"

Levana leaned forward, her eyes gleaming with a twisted sense of satisfaction. "My freedom. You let me walk out of here, and I'll give you the antidote."

Petunia was stunned at this. Let Levana go free? After everything she had done? After she had killed her own husband, infected innocent people, and endangered Diana's life?

But then she thought of the citizens—weak, feverish, barely able to breathe with rashes all over their bodies. The doctors had said there was nothing they could do. Without the antidote, they would die, including Diana.

"Petunia...you can't," Zain's voice came through the earpiece. He and the rest of the team were listening from the observation room, watching every second unfold. "She's bluffing."

But Petunia wasn't so sure. Levana had planned every move so methodically—could she really be bluffing now?

"I'll give you five seconds to make your decision," Levana said, her smile widening. "After that, the antidote will be gone forever. One...."

"Don't do it," Sophia's voice urged. "We'll find another way."

"Two."

Petunia's mind raced. Could she risk it? Could she gamble with the city's lives?

"Three."

She clenched her fists. Diana. Sweet, innocent Diana and the lovely people of Furors; Petunia couldn't let them die.

"Four."

With a heavy heart, Petunia made her choice.

"Fine," she said, her voice barely more than a whisper. "You walk, and I get the antidote."

Levana's grin spread wider. "Smart choice."

Petunia felt a surge of disgust wash over her. She wanted nothing more than to wipe that smirk off Levana's face, but right now, the people were all that mattered.

"Where is it?" Petunia demanded.

Levana paused, savouring the moment. "There's a vial. Hidden inside the necklace I was wearing when you arrested me. The one you confiscated."

Petunia blinked in shock. Could it really be that simple? Levana had worn the antidote around her neck the entire time?

"You'll find it in the evidence locker," Levana continued. "But don't take too long. That infection works fast."

Petunia turned, ready to storm out of the room and retrieve the vial. But Levana's voice stopped her in her tracks.

"Just remember," Levana said softly, her voice dripping with malice, "even if you save them, you'll never truly win. I've already set things in motion that you can't stop." Petunia didn't respond. She couldn't. She sprang into action.

She rushed to the evidence room along with her devastated team, her hands shaking as she rifled through the confiscated items. And then, she saw it—the necklace. Her breath caught in her throat as she carefully opened the pendant.

Inside, just as Levana had promised, was a small vial filled with a clear liquid. The antidote.

With trembling hands, Petunia grabbed it and they contacted the lab to produce similar vaccines. In no time, there were vials enough to treat all the infected people. The doctors worked quickly, administering the antidotes while the team stood by.

Petunia stayed close to Diana. For what felt like an eternity, she watched as she lay motionless, her breathing shallow. And then, slowly, her eyes fluttered open.

"Mom?" Diana's voice was weak, but it was the most beautiful sound Petunia had ever heard.

Tears filled Petunia's eyes as she knelt by her daughter's side. "I'm here, sweetheart. I'm here."

Diana smiled faintly, her hand reaching out to grasp Petunia's. "You saved me."

Petunia's heart filled with relief. "Yes, dear. I saved you."

But even as she held her daughter's hand, a dark shadow lingered in the back of her mind. Levana had warned her—this wasn't over. The infection may have been stopped, but there were still more pieces to this puzzle. And Petunia knew that as long as Levana was out there, the city would never truly be safe.

# CHAPTER 5

# PEACE

Panic buzzed in the air. Levana's warning still echoed in Petunia's mind.

*"This isn't over."*

As the days passed, Petunia found it harder to shake the feeling that something worse was coming. She barely slept; her thoughts consumed by the possibility of Levana's schemes still unfolding in the shadows. The city may have been saved for now, but what about the world?

The news confirmed her worst fears. Reports started flooding in from nearby nations—Franca, Beligia, Suncham, and Litnich. People were falling ill, showing the same symptoms as those infected in Furors. The infection had spread.

Petunia stood in the briefing room, staring at the map, now lit up with red dots where the infection had appeared. "We should have known this wasn't limited to one place," Hiroshi said, "Levana had more reach than we imagined."

"She's been planning this for years," Petunia exclaimed, "This was never just about our city."

"At least we have the antidote now," one of the medics chimed in. "We can produce it in large quantities and send it to the affected nations."

Petunia nodded, "The antidote might not be enough. Levana could have more tricks up her sleeve."

The team sprang into action, coordinating with medical units across the neighbouring countries. Vials of the antidote were rushed to Franca, Beligia, Suncham, and Litnich, with doctors and medics on high alert.

But as the hours dragged on, the infection continued to spread at an alarming rate. Terror surged through the streets of those nations as people scrambled for answers, desperate to protect their families.

Petunia's phone buzzed. A message from the lab.

"New strains detected. We might be dealing with mutations."

Her blood ran cold. Levana had anticipated their every move. The infection had evolved, and now even the antidote seemed fragile against its power.

By the time Petunia arrived at the hospital, the atmosphere was tense. Doctors and nurses moved in frantic waves, administering antidotes to the new patients flooding the emergency rooms. Outside, helicopters roared overhead, carrying vials to neighbouring nations as fast as they could.

Petunia spotted the head scientist from the lab, Dr. Monroe, huddled with a group of specialists. She rushed toward them.

"What's the situation?" she demanded, trying to mask the fear clawing at her chest.

Dr. Monroe looked up, his face pale with exhaustion. "We've got new data. The infection is mutating faster than we expected. But the antidote is holding—so far."

"How long until we know for sure?"

"Another 24 hours. If we're lucky."

Petunia nodded, "Keep me updated doctor."

As she turned to leave, her phone buzzed again, but this time, it wasn't from the lab. It was from Levana. She had chosen to call Petunia herself now.

*"I'm done with what I had to do and now, I'm coming for you. It's time you meet your end. See me where it all began, let's end this."*

The place where it all began was the lab where the infection had first been developed. Levana was calling her out, one final showdown. Petunia knew she couldn't ignore it. She had to end this.

The abandoned lab stood at the edge of the city, surrounded by a barren wasteland where nature had started to reclaim the ruins.

The team insisted on coming with her and as they approached the building, an odd silence settled over the air. No sign of Levana, no traps, no chaos. Just stillness.

"Stay close," Petunia whispered to her team. Her pulse raced as they entered the building, the once-bustling lab now a haunting relic of the past.

They moved through the abandoned half-burnt corridors, their footsteps echoing. And then, in the centre of the main room, they saw her.

Levana stood alone, dressed in all black, her expression relaxed as usual. The lab's large shattered glass windows cast distorted shadows across the floor. In her hand, she held a small vial—the antidote for the mutation.

"So glad you could make it," Levana said, her voice smooth and perilous.

"Where's the rest of your army?" Petunia asked, her voice steady despite the fear gnawing at her insides.

Levana smirked. "I don't need an army. This isn't about them. This is about us, Petunia."

Petunia stepped forward, her eyes locked on Levana's. "You need to stop this. You've done enough damage. The infection—"

"—is a masterpiece," Levana interrupted, her smile widening. "It's far more than an infection. It's a weapon of control. Something no one else could have created."

"You're destroying lives!" Petunia snapped, her voice rising with emotion. "You're playing with people's futures, with their families, their children!"

Levana's eyes rolled with something almost like boredom. "Spare me the morality lecture. I did what had to be done. This city, this world... it was broken long before I came along. All I did was accelerate the process. That's all. Wasn't the world bound to end anyways?"

Sophia stepped forward, her hand resting on the gun holstered at her hip. "Levana, this is over. Put the vial down."

Levana laughed, the sound sharp and cold. "Over? Oh, darling, this is just the beginning. But if you want this," she said, holding up the vial, "you'll have to take it from me."

Petunia lunged forward, but Levana was fast, pulling out a small device from her pocket. Before Petunia could react, Levana pressed a button, and a series of explosions ripped through the lab once again.

The ground shook violently, sending Petunia and the team crashing to the floor. Smoke filled the room as debris rained down, the remains of the chipped walls crashing under the force of the blast.

Petunia coughed, struggling to her feet as she searched for Levana through the haze. But she was gone.

"Team! Is everyone good?" Petunia called, panic rising in her throat.

"We're okay!" their voices came from somewhere nearby. "We need to get out of here, now!"

But Petunia wasn't ready to give up. Not yet. She stumbled through the wreckage, her heart pounding as she searched for any sign of Levana.

And then, through the smoke, she saw her. Levana was slipping through a side door, the vial still clutched in her hand.

Without a second thought, Petunia raced after her. The two women burst out into the open air. Levana was fast, but Petunia was one step ahead of her. She tackled Levana to the ground, wrestling the vial from her hand. Levana fought back, but Petunia was stronger. She pinned Levana down. "It's over, darling," Petunia smiled.

Levana laughed, even as blood trickled from the corner of her mouth. "You think you've won? You haven't stopped anything. The infection is still out there. And without me, you'll never control it."

Petunia's grip tightened on the vial. "We'll find a way."

Levana's eyes gleamed with malevolence. "Ha! You'll never get rid of me, Petunia. Even if you kill me, I'll haunt you forever."

Petunia didn't respond. She didn't need to. She had the antidote, and Levana was done for.

Petunia's team arrived seconds later, cuffing Levana and leading her away. As they drove off, Petunia stared down at the vial in her hand. It was the key to saving the rest of the world.

The infection was stopped in the nearby nations, thanks to the scientists and medics who successfully replicated the antidote and distributed it to all affected nations. Levana was arrested and taken into custody. But the fear she had spread—would never be forgotten.

The city had survived. But as Petunia watched Levana disappear into the distance, she knew the battle for peace had only just begun.

**Is this war really over?**

# Author's Note

Hi there! I'm Afsheen Sheikh and I'm fourteen years old from Abu Dhabi. I enjoy doing art, writing, volunteering and baking, and occasionally play the piano. I believe creativity is my biggest strength and I can use my potential to make our world a better place for everyone.

Over the past three years, I have dedicated myself to improving my writing skills and publishing 6 other books, and I'm excited to finally share the release of the 2nd book in my series, *Petunia Wolf - The Case Cracker*. This journey has been incredibly rewarding, allowing me to delve deeper into the art of storytelling and character development. I hope that you find as much enjoyment in reading it as I did in writing it.

I invite you to explore my other works available on Amazon *(Petunia Wolf Book-1, Living in Nature's Arms, Brainy Bliss, The Enchanting Yarn of Tales, Poetry Metropolis and my Hindi book which holds the World Book of Records title of being written by the Youngest Hindi Author, अद्वि और अन्वि के मज़ेदार किस्से)* where you can discover more of my stories and adventures. Your support means the world to me, and I am thrilled to continue sharing my passion for storytelling and writing with you.